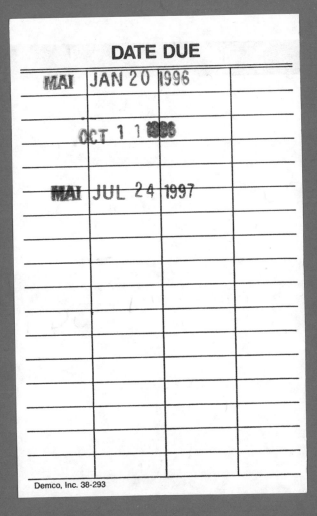

DATE DUE

MAI	JAN 20 1996	
	OCT 1 1 1996	
MAI	JUL 24 1997	

Demco, Inc. 38-293

HOW
IWARIWA THE CAYMAN
LEARNED TO SHARE

A YANOMAMI MYTH

VENEZUELA

SOUTH AMERICA

BRAZIL

PACIFIC
OCEAN

ATLANTIC
OCEAN

● YANOMAMI AREA

HOW
IWARIWA THE CAYMAN
LEARNED TO SHARE

A YANOMAMI MYTH RETOLD AND ILLUSTRATED BY

GEORGE CRESPO

CLARION BOOKS
NEW YORK

I wish to acknowledge Bobby Gonzalez
and the staff of the Huntington Free Library
for their ongoing support.

CLARION BOOKS
a Houghton Mifflin Company imprint
215 Park Avenue South, New York, NY 10003
Text and illustrations copyright © 1995 by George Crespo

Book design by Sylvia Frezzolini Severance
Illustrations executed in oils on rag paper
Text is 16-point Garamond No. 3

Printed in the USA

Library of Congress Cataloging-in-Publication Data

Crespo, George.
    How Iwariwa the cayman learned to share / a Yanomami myth
retold and illustrated by George Crespo.   p.   cm.
    Summary: The animals in the Amazon rainforest find a way to trick
Iwariwa the cayman into sharing the fire he uses to cook his food.
      ISBN 0-395-67162-0
      1. Yanomamo Indians—Folklore.   2. Tales—Venezuela.
[1. Yanomamo Indians—Folklore.   2. Indians of South America—Folklore.
3. Folklore—Venezuela. 4. Fire—Folklore.]   I. Title.
F2520.1.Y3C74   1995
398.2'089982—dc20
[E]   94-14212   CIP   AC

HOR 10 9 8 7 6 5 4 3 2 1

This book is dedicated to my grandfathers,
Abuelo Toto and Abuelo Juan Luis,
who have already passed on.

A long, long time ago, say the Yanomami people, before human beings came to the Amazon rain forest, animals could talk. They cooked their food over a fire, as people do. But there was a time before that when the animals didn't even know about fire, and they ate their food raw.

Every evening, as the forest cooled down, the animals would gather in their *maloca*, their village hut, to share stories over their evening meal. They ate raw root vegetables, which were hard and chewy. But the animals didn't mind, because they didn't know that food could taste any different.

One evening, Kanaporiwa the bird told them about something exciting she had seen that day. "When I flew over the hut of Iwariwa the cayman, I saw a wispy cloud coming up from the opening in the roof. As I flew closer, I saw Iwariwa's wife, Pruwaheiyoma, bent over a strange orange heat that danced as though it were alive and gave off a crackling sound. She poked around in the dancing heat with a stick and pulled out sweet potatoes that were crisp and brown on the outside. Iwariwa took them from her and broke them open, and I heard him tell Pruwaheiyoma how sweet and tasty they were as he stuffed them in his mouth. The smell was delectable, let me tell you."

"What is this wondrous heat that makes *hukomo* so delicious?" asked Dihi the jaguar.

"Iwariwa called it fire, and he told Pruwaheiyoma to make sure no one finds out he has it. I know where he keeps it, though. After he and Pruwaheiyoma finished eating, I saw Iwariwa put the fire in a little magic basket and hide the basket in his mouth."

"That's not fair," said Pasho the spider monkey. "Iwariwa

should give us some of the fire. We've always shared our food with him. Why should he be the only one to know how to make it hot and delicious?"

"If we can find a way to make Iwariwa open his mouth," said Dihi the jaguar, "one of us could easily grab his little magic basket. Then we could all share the fire. So let us find a way to make Iwariwa laugh." And the animals came up with a plan.

The next morning Dihi went to visit Iwariwa. As he approached the caymans' hut, he heard Pruwaheiyoma complaining to her husband. "We never see anyone," she said. "We just stay home so you can guard the fire. Sometimes I wish you had never found that tree struck by lightning." Dihi could see Iwariwa sitting in his hammock, listening, with his mouth closed.

Dihi called out at the hut's entrance, and Pruwaheiyoma came to the opening. "We're having a feast in four days' time," Dihi told her, "and you and Iwariwa are invited to be the guests of honor."

"Thank you," said Pruwaheiyoma. "If Iwariwa agrees, we will be there."

As Dihi watched closely, Iwariwa took something small from his mouth and held it behind his back. "Of course we'll come to the party," said Iwariwa. As he spoke, three rings of smoke rose from his snout. Pretending not to notice, Dihi took his leave.

The caymans arrived at the party dressed in their best. Everyone ate delicious papaya—everyone but Iwariwa, who kept his mouth shut tight.

After the refreshments, Dihi asked the guests to be seated for the evening's entertainment. "Yarime the capuchin monkey will balance four gourds filled with water," he said.

Everyone but Iwariwa cheered as Yarime and his assistant, Tepe the anteater, stepped forward. Tepe clicked his bow and arrows together, *Prrrrrrrrrrrt!* as the capuchin monkey carefully raised a wooden contraption that held four large gourds and placed it on his nose.

At once the wooden frame began to wobble. "Oh, oh, oh!" cried Yarime, weaving comically from side to side. The gourds came tumbling down, drenching the unsuspecting anteater with water.

Everyone laughed—everyone but Iwariwa, who smiled politely.

Tepe the anteater jumped up and ran around the *maloca*, shaking off the water and making faces. All the guests laughed as they were sprinkled with water—all but Iwariwa.

Then Tepe pretended to slip. He tripped, rolled over, did a cartwheel, and fell flat on his back. At this Iwariwa smiled, then grinned. The other animals held their breath—it was now or never!

At last Iwariwa let out a thunderous guffaw. The little basket came shooting out of his mouth and into the sky, trailing smoke like a tiny comet.

Kanaporiwa the bird, who had been waiting on a branch nearby, took off and snatched the basket in midair.

"No!" shouted Iwariwa. "That's mine!" He jumped up and chased after her.

With Iwariwa crashing through the forest in pursuit, Kanaporiwa flew to the riverbank. There she passed the magic basket to Totori the tortoise. The tortoise hid the basket in her shell and swam off across the river as fast as she could, with Iwariwa close behind, snapping his jaws.

On the other side of the river, Opo the armadillo was waiting. Totori gave him the little basket. He hid it in his armor, then—as the furious cayman came storming up onto the riverbank—he began to dig a tunnel.

Iwariwa the cayman dove right into the tunnel after Opo, but it was only wide enough for an armadillo, and Iwariwa got stuck halfway in. The more he struggled and lashed his tail, the more firmly he wedged himself in the hole—just as the other animals had planned.

"Help!" he called as the others gathered. "Get me out of here!"

"And what about the fire?" demanded Dihi. "Will you let the rest of us have some?"

"Yes! Yes!" cried Iwariwa. "Only get me out of here, and I will share the fire with all of you!"

The other animals dug and scratched and pulled him free, and from then on they all ate sweet, delicious *hukomo* cooked over their fires.

This all happened long, long ago. Since that time, the Yanomami people say, the animals have gotten out of the habit of using fire. But when people are sitting around a fire, sometimes they see eyes shining in the bushes and among the tree branches. The animals come to gaze proudly at the fire they still think of as theirs, because they helped get it from Iwariwa the cayman.

A NOTE

The Yanomami (sometimes written Yanomamo or Yanomama) live in the Amazon rain forest areas of southern Venezuela and northern Brazil. *How Iwariwa the Cayman Learned to Share* is a retelling of their theft-of-fire myth, a traditional tale featuring myth-age animals who could speak.

The Yanomami people rely on gardening for most of their food. From their village gardens, located near the communal dwellings called *malocas*, they harvest a variety of produce including plantain, fruits like papaya, and root vegetables such as manioc and sweet potatoes or *hukomo*, many of which are prepared by roasting. They also eat thumb-sized larvae found in fallen palm tree trunks; in some versions of this story, remains of roasted larvae under the cayman's hammock reveal his secret.

Feasts are important occasions for the Yanomami, serving to strengthen relations between the host village and the guests. In preparation for the festivities the people decorate themselves with feathers and paint designs on their faces and bodies with vegetable pigments such as red annatto-seed paste.

At one time the largest, least acculturated group in the Americas, the Yanomami today may number twenty thousand. They maintain their traditional way of life with increasing difficulty. Although the Yanomami homeland was recognized by the Brazilian government in 1992 and the Venezuelan government has set aside a large tract of land for the Yanomami, illegal gold mining in their territory and forced contact with Western society have placed the Yanomami's survival as a people at risk. Individuals and organizations worldwide are working to preserve the cultures of the Amazon peoples and the irreplaceable environment that is their home.

My retelling of the story is based on three sources: Napoleon A. Chagnon, *Yanomamo: The Fierce People* (second edition. Holt, Rinehart and Winston, 1968, 1977) and *Yanomamo: The Last Days of Eden* (Harcourt Brace Jovanovich, 1992); and Maria Isabel Eguillor Garcia, *Yopo, shamanes, y hekura: aspectos fenomenologicos del mundo sagrado yanomami* (Libreria Editorial Salesiana, 1984). In some versions of the story, the hummingbird steals the fire and deposits it high in the branches of a certain tree; this is said to explain why certain kinds of wood can be used to start fires with. Sometimes the cayman keeps hot embers, rather than a flame, in his mouth, which explains why the inside of a cayman's mouth is red. I added the "relay race" in which the fire is passed from one animal to another in order to include more indigenous animals in the story. I also added the magic basket to make it plausible for Iwariwa to keep the flame in his mouth for so long.

I am grateful to anthropologist Gale Goodwin Gomez for her advice on the story and on the pronunciation of Yanomami names. The Yanomami language contains vowel sounds not found in English; suggested pronunciations are approximate.

Dihi	DIH hih	Pasho	PA sho
hukomo	hoo KO mo	Pruwaheiyoma	proo wah hey YO mah
Iwariwa	ee wah REE wah	Tepe	TUH puh
Kanaporiwa	kah nah po REE wah	Totori	toe TOE ree
maloca	mah LO kah	Yanomami	yah no MAH mee
Opo	OH po	Yarime	yahr EEM uh